WE SHALL ALL BE FREE:

Survivors of Racism

Survivors: Ordinary People, Extaordinary Circumstances

An Enemy Within:
Overcoming Cancer and Other Life-Threatening Diseases

Danger in the Deep:
Surviving Shark Attacks

Gender Danger:
Survivors of Rape, Human Trafficking, and Honor Killings

In Defense of Our Country:
Survivors of Military Conflict

Lost!
Surviving in the Wilderness

Nature's Wrath:
Surviving Natural Disasters

Never Again:
Survivors of the Holocaust

Students in Danger:
Survivors of School Violence

Survival Skills:
How to Handle Life's Catastrophes

Those Who Remain:
What It Means to Be a Survivor

We Shall All Be Free:
Survivors of Racism

When Danger Hits Home:
Survivors of Domestic Violence

The World Gone Mad:
Surviving Acts of Terrorism

WE SHALL ALL BE FREE:

Survivors of Racism

Ellyn Sanna

 Mason Crest Publishers

WE SHALL ALL BE FREE: Survivors of Racism

MASON CREST PUBLISHERS INC.
370 Reed Road
Broomall, Pennsylvania 19008
(866)MCP-BOOK (toll free)
www.masoncrest.com

Because the stories in this series are told by real people, in some cases names have been changed to protect the privacy of the individuals.

First Printing
9 8 7 6 5 4 3 2 1

ISBN 978-1-4222-0449-8 (series)
ISBN 978-1-4222-1462-6 (series) (pbk.)

Library of Congress Cataloging-in-Publication Data

Sanna, Ellyn, 1957–
CIP data on file at the Library of Congress.

Design by MK Bassett-Harvey.
Produced by Harding House Publishing Service, Inc.
www.hardinghousepages.com
Cover design by Wendy Arakawa.
Printed in The Hashimite Kingdom of Jordan.

CONTENTS

Introduction

Each of us is confronted with challenges and hardships in our daily lives. Some of us, however, have faced extraordinary challenges and severe adversity. Those who have lived—and often thrived—through affliction, illness, pain, tragedy, cruelty, fear, and even near-death experiences are known as survivors. We have much to learn from survivors and much to admire.

Survivors fascinate us. Notice how many books, movies, and television shows focus on individuals facing—and overcoming—extreme situations. *Robinson Crusoe* is probably the earliest example of this, followed by books like the *Swiss Family Robinson*. Even the old comedy *Gilligan's Island* appealed to this fascination, and today we have everything from the Tom Hanks' movie *Castaway* to the hit reality show *Survivor* and the popular TV show *Lost*.

What is it about survivors that appeals so much to us? Perhaps it's the message of hope they give us. These people have endured extreme challenges—and they've overcome them. They're ordinary people who faced extraordinary situations. And if they can do it, just maybe we can too.

This message is an appropriate one for young adults. After all, adolescence is a time of daily challenges. Change is everywhere in their lives, demanding that they adapt and cope with a constantly shifting reality. Their bodies change in response to increasing levels of sex hormones; their thinking processes change as their brains develop, allowing them to think in more abstract ways; their social lives change as new people and peers become more important. Suddenly, they experience the burning need to form their own identities. At the same time, their emotions are labile and unpredictable. The people they were as children may seem to have disappeared beneath the onslaught of new emotions, thoughts, and sensations. Young adults have to deal with every single one of these changes, all at the same time. Like many of the survivors whose stories are told in this series, adolescents' reality is often a frightening, confusing, and unfamiliar place.

Young adults are in crises that are no less real simply because these are crises we all live through (and most of us survive!) Like all survivors, young adults emerge from their crises transformed; they are not the people they were before. Many of them bear scars they will carry with them for life—and yet these scars can be integrated into their new identities. Scars may even become sources of strength.

In this book series, young adults will have opportunities to learn from individuals faced with tremendous struggles. Each individual has her own story, her own set of circumstances and challenges, and her own way of coping and surviving. Whether facing cancer or abuse, terrorism or natural disaster, genocide or school violence, all the survivors who tell their stories in this series have found the ability and will to carry on despite the trauma. They cope, persevere, persist, and live on as a person changed forever by the ordeal and suffering they endured. They offer hope and wisdom to young adults: if these people can do it, so can they!

These books offer a broad perspective on life and its challenges. They will allow young readers to become more self-aware of the demanding and difficult situations in their own lives—while at the same time becoming more compassionate toward those who have gone through the unthinkable traumas that occur in our world.

— Andrew M. Kleiman, M.D.

Chapter One

STRANGERS IN A STRANGE LAND

Mae-Ann Smith lives in a trailer. (In the rural English village where Mae-Ann lives, the trailer is called a caravan). She lives there not because she can't afford a house, but because, for Mae-Ann, living in a trailer is an **affirmation** of her cultural identity. She and her people are not House-Dwellers. They're Travelers.

affirmation: confirming that something is true; giving a positive assessment.

You may have never heard of Mae-Ann's people. If you have, you may think of them as Gypsies. Some people call them Roma. People have hated and feared them for centuries. Mae-Ann has faced racism her entire life.

HISTORY LESSON

The Roma are an ancient ethnic group. From the beginning of their history, they have absorbed many groups, welcoming into their midst all who lived their lives on the road, **nomads** who traveled from place to place rather than settling down on a particular spot of land.

nomads: people with no permanent home who move from place to place.

When the Roma first arrived in Europe in the 1300s, Europeans knew only that they came from the East. Back then, Europeans weren't too clear on geography; one of the few places they knew that lay to the East was Egypt, so they called these dark-eyed, dark-haired strangers Egyptians or 'Gyptians—and eventually, this turned into "Gypsy."

In fact, however, the Roma people came from India. Their native language still shares many words with the Indian language called Sanskrit. Historians now believe the Roma left India a thousand years ago, at the beginning of the eleventh century, when conflicts between Islam and Hinduism pushed them out of their home. As they moved northwestward through Persia, they picked up words and grammar from the Persian language—and no doubt absorbed new members too. The same thing happened as they traveled on into Armenia and then into the Byzantine Empire. In time, they reached Europe, and by 1500, the Roma had spread all the way to the farthest corners of that continent.

A traditional Roma caravan. Some Roma in parts of Europe still travel in these beautifully decorated wagons.

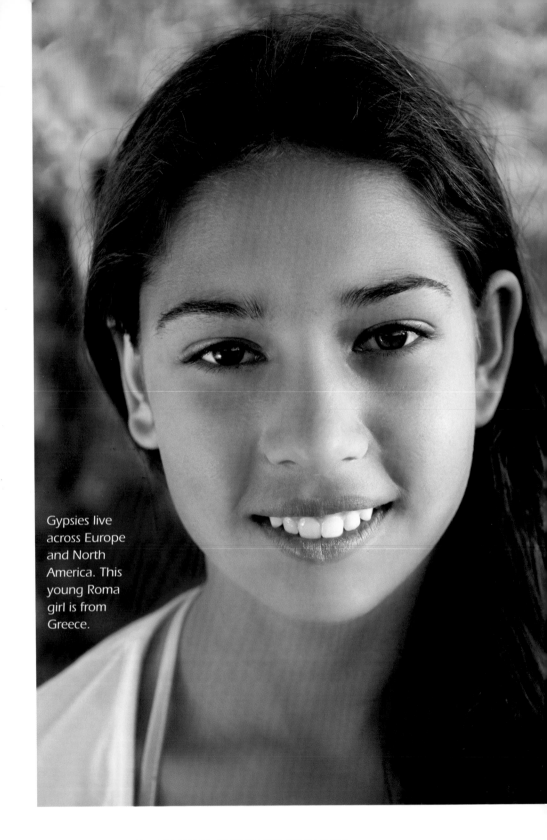

Gypsies live across Europe and North America. This young Roma girl is from Greece.

But they never settled down in one place. For one thing, no one made them welcome. They were strangers. They looked different. They spoke a different language. They had different customs. All these differences scared the people who lived in the countries where they traveled. Racism raised its ugly head.

WHAT CAUSES RACISM?

Racism is rooted in prejudice, and the root word of prejudice is "pre-judge." Prejudiced people often judge others based purely on their race or ethnic group; they make assumptions about others that may have no basis in reality. They believe that if your skin is darker or you speak a different language or wear different clothes or worship God in a different way, then they already know you are not as smart, not as nice, not as honest, not as valuable, or not as moral as they are.

sociologists: people who study human societies and their organizations and institutions.

Why do human beings have these feelings? **Sociologists** believe humans have a

High School Stereotypes

The average high school has its share of stereotypes—lumping a certain kind of person together, ignoring all the ways that each person is unique. These stereotypes are often expressed with a single word or phrase: "jock," "nerd," "goth," "prep," or "geek." The images these words call to mind are easily recognized and understood by others who share the same views.

Where Are the Roots of Prejudice?

Sociologists have found that people who are prejudiced toward one group of people also tend to be prejudiced toward other groups. In a study done in 1946, people were asked about their attitudes concerning a variety of ethnic groups, including Danireans, Pirraneans, and Wallonians. The study found that people who were prejudiced toward blacks and Jews also distrusted these other three groups. The catch is that Danireans, Pirraneans, and Wallonians didn't exist! This suggests that prejudice's existence may be rooted within the person who feels prejudice rather than in the group that is feared and hated.

basic tendency to fear anything that's unfamiliar or unknown. Someone who is strange (in that they're not like us) is scary; they're automatically dangerous or inferior. If we get to know the strangers, of course, we end up discovering that they're not so different from ourselves; they're not so frightening and threatening after all. But too often, we don't let that happen. We put up a wall between the strangers and ourselves. We're on the inside; they're on the outside. And then we peer over the wall, too far away from the people on the other side to see anything but our differences.

over-simplification: to simplify something to the point where the truth becomes obscured or misrepresented.

Here's where another human tendency comes into play: stereotyping. A stereotype is a fixed, commonly held notion or image of a person or group that's based on an **oversimplification** of some observed or imagined trait. Stereotypes assume that whatever is believed about a group is typical for each individual within that group.

Most stereotypes tend to make us feel superior in some way to the person or group being stereotyped. Not all stereotypes are negative, however; some are positive—"black men are good at basketball" or "Asian students are smart"—but that doesn't make them true. They ignore individuals' uniqueness. They make assumptions that may or may not be accurate.

We can't help our human tendency to put people into categories. As babies, we faced

Six Characteristics of a Racial Minority Group

1. Minority group members suffer oppression at the hands of another group.
2. A minority group is identified by certain traits that are clearly visible and obvious.
3. Minorities see themselves as belonging to a special and separate social unit; they identify with others like themselves.
4. A person does not voluntarily become a member of a minority; he or she is born into it.
5. Members of racial minority groups usually don't marry outside the group. If intermarriage is high, ethnic identities and loyalties are weakening.
6. "Minority" is a social, not a numerical concept. In other words, it doesn't matter how many members of a particular "out-group" live in a region compared to the "in-group"; what matters are who has the power and social prestige.

Four Characteristics of Racial Prejudice

1. a feeling of superiority
2. a feeling that the minority is different and alien
3. a feeling of rightful claim to power, privilege, and status
4. a fear and suspicion that the minority wants to take the power, privilege, and status from the dominant group

a confusing world filled with an amazing variety of new things. We needed a way to make sense of it all, so one of our first steps in learning about the world around us was to sort things into separate slots in our heads: small furry things that said *meow* were kitties, while larger furry things that said *arf-arf* were doggies; cars went *vroom-vroom*, but trains were longer and go *choo-choo*; little girls looked one way and little boys another; and doctors wore white coats, while police officers wore blue. These were our earliest stereotypes. They were a handy way to make sense of the world; they helped us know what to expect, so that each time we faced a new person or thing, we weren't starting all over again from scratch. But stereotypes become dangerous when we continue to hold onto our mental images despite new evidence. (For instance, as a child you may have decided that all dogs bite—which

Gypsies brought with them on their travels India's love of decoration and color.

Group Pressure

Why do people continue to believe stereotypes despite evidence that may not support them? Researchers have found that it may have something to do with group pressure. During one experiment, seven members of a group were asked to state that a short line is longer than a long line. About a third of the rest of the group agreed that the short line was longer, despite evidence to the contrary. Apparently, people conform to the beliefs of those around them in order to gain group acceptance.

means that when faced by friendly, harmless dogs, you assume they're dangerous and so you miss out on getting to know all dogs.) Stereotypes are particularly dangerous and destructive when they're directed at persons or groups of persons. That's when they turn into prejudice.

But prejudice alone doesn't necessarily equal racism. Prejudice is an attitude, a way of looking at the world. When it turns into action it's called discrimination. Discrimination is when people are treated differently (and unfairly) because they belong to a particular group of people. Prejudice may be the root of racism—but discrimination is its branches and leaves.

MAE-ANN'S STORY

Being a Traveler is important to Mae-Ann. It's who she is, it's who her parents were, and it's who she wants her children to be. But she hates the fact that people hate her and her children simply because of who they are.

"Some people choose to live on the farmland they inherited from their families versus moving to the city," she said. "They want to live close to the land and keep their lifestyle simple. What if those people were hated and looked down on, simply because of how and where they choose to live? No one does that, of course. But they don't see that how they treat gypsies is the same thing."

Mae-Ann explains that the laws in the United Kingdom have made it difficult for her people to live their traditional lifestyle. "We can't move around anymore like we used to. Now there are laws that say we can't set up our camps on the land where we always did. So we're forced to either break the law—or buy land and set up permanent camps. But even then, towns don't want us. They tell us we can't live here. They take advantage of loopholes in the law and push us out. What are we supposed to do? They want to destroy us, so we don't know who we are anymore.

"My daughter has blonde hair. You can't tell by looking at her that she's Gypsy.

Ethnocentrism

Ethnocentrism refers to a tendency to view one's own ethnic group's behaviors as "normal." Other groups are not only viewed as different, but they are seen as strange and sometimes inferior.

What makes her different is that she's not a House-Dweller. I want her to know who she is. I want her to live with her people. But people around here don't want that. So

I have to choose—do I want my daughter to grow up knowing who she is? Or do I want her to grow up being accepted by the other children in her school? I shouldn't have to

In England, some Gypsies today live in these kinds of caravans. But it is hard for them to travel around as they once did, since land is not available for them to use when they stop.

Traveler History

After the bombs of World War II, many people were left homeless in England. Traveler groups absorbed thousands of these individuals into their communities. Today, in the United Kingdom, the Gypsy and Traveler community is made up of people of Roma descent, along with Irish Travelers and other Traveler groups. UK officials estimate that 90,000 to 120,000 Gypsies and Travelers still live the traditional nomadic life in their country, while another 200,000 have been forced to settle down and live in permanent housing of some form. Their exact numbers are hard to determine for certain, since they are not recorded on UK census records.

make that choice. But my people and I aren't welcome in this country. We're not welcome anywhere. We've been hated and driven out for the last thousand years."

Mae-Ann isn't exaggerating her situation. Her story is being acted out again and again across the United Kingdom. For instance, the residents of one English village built walls of concrete blocks and mud to keep Gypsies from the land they had bought for their caravans.

The group of Travelers had bought the field at the edge of town in 2001. They'd put in water and electricity, built cement foundations for their caravans, and created driveways. By the next year, twenty-some families were living there. They thought they'd done everything right. They didn't realize they had failed to submit one essential piece of paperwork to the town government.

In 2004, the town's **bailiffs**, backed by a hundred police officers, forced the community's residents out of their homes. Townspeople got involved; fights broke out; people were injured; and one caravan was set on fire and destroyed.

"The families who were here have been traveling around the country just trying to find somewhere to stay," a member of the Gypsy Council told a BBC reporter. "If people can't live on their own land they end

bailiffs:
in Britain officers who assist the sheriff and have the authority to collect fines or make arrests.

This Travelers' community in Shropshire, England, is much like the one where Mae-Ann lives.

What Do the Roma Have in Common?

The Roma culture varies from group to group, but all Roma share some things in common: loyalty to family (extended and clan); belief in *Del* (God) and *beng* (the Devil); belief that each of our destinies is laid out for us ahead of time. As different groups have been absorbed into the Roma population in a particular area, some Roma traditions and beliefs have been watered down or changed. This means that it's impossible to stereotype the Roma people; you can't say, "All Gypsies are like this. . ." even in the most general terms.

up living illegally on other people's plots or illegally by the road side."

Of course, each story always has two sides. The village government insisted its actions had nothing to do with discrimination, that it was merely applying a law that protects rural landscapes from development. The townspeople supported this view. They did not want the Gypsy community in their village because of the noise, illegal dumping, and vandalism the Gypsies brought with them (according to the villagers). When a BBC reported asked a resident if he had actually met any of the **evicted** Gypsies, he responded, "Are you serious? They were just not normal. Clash of cultures has nothing to do with it. If anyone had 15 families moving next door to them they would feel **intimidated**." The local authorities also claimed that they'd already done their part on behalf of Gypsies: the village has an existing, approved Travelers' caravan not far from the illegal site.

evicted:
put out.

intimidated:
filled with fear,
due to threats
or the force
of another's
personality.

This Roma woman looks more like our stereotypes of a "Gypsy," but many modern Roma and Travelers are blonde-haired and light-skinned.

What do you think?

Did the village's actions show discrimination against Gypsies? Why or why not?

When you walk through this official site, you find a well-kept trailer park that's home to ten families. All the plots are taken, and no one sounds like they're planning to move, so clearly, this site will do the evicted Gypsies no good. The residents say their kids attend the local schools, and they don't want to move for fear they won't find anywhere else to "stop" legally. The residents also say they try not to draw attention to themselves. One resident told the BBC reporter, "The [villagers] may talk about [garbage dumping] from the other community but our experience is different. I have been woken up by cars from who knows where emptying rubbish on to our back field. Who do you think gets the blame?"

"This just the way it goes if you're a Traveler," Mae-Ann said. "You don't even feel surprised or outraged when you hear stories like this. It's just what you expect. And I think that's the saddest thing—that we just take it, that we accept it, like it's a fact of life we can't change."

Mae-Ann looked across the trailer park that's her home. Two little girls peeked out the window of the trailer across the lane, then quickly disappeared. Mae-Ann smiled, but she looked sad. "Our children deserve the same things from life that anyone else does. Instead, we have pedophiles hanging around our communities, thinking our children are the sort no one cares about, that no one will miss. And when we call the police, no one cares, no one comes."

Finding an Identity

Today, the Roma are working to achieve an identity recognized by the nations of the world. They have their own international symbol—a spoked-wheel that represents a sixteen-spoked *chakra* (a link to the Roma's Indian origins that represents movement and the original Creation); their own green and blue flag with a red chakra in the center; their own motto—*Opré Roma* (*Roma Arise*); their own anthem; and their own International Romani Day—April 8. The World Romani Congress meets to work for standardizing the Roma language, reparations from World War II, improvements in civil rights and education, preservation of the Roma culture, and international recognition of the Roma as a minority of Indian origin. Another Roma organization, the International Romani Union, has consultative status to the United Nations Social and Economic Council.

The green and blue flag from 1933, now embellished with the red, sixteen-spoked chakra, was reaffirmed as the national emblem of the Romani people at the first World Romani Congress in 1971.

Another Group of Wanderers

Like Gypsies, the Jews have often been forced to travel from country to country, never welcomed—and like the Gypsies, the Jews have survived centuries of prejudice.

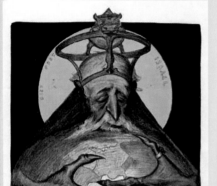

There's even a special word for this kind of prejudice: anti-Semitism.

Over the years, anti-Semitism has shown up in many ways that range from individual expressions of discrimination against individual Jews, to organized government-sponsored violent attacks on entire Jewish communities. During the Middle Ages in Europe, for example, Jews were thrown out of their homes, forced to convert to Christianity, or even killed. In 1096, the Jewish communities along Germany's Rhine and Danube rivers were completely destroyed. During the Crusades, as Christians tried to capture their "Holy Land," Jews in France were frequently massacred, while in England and Austria, they were banished. During the fourteenth century, as the Black Death swept through Europe, Jews were often the scapegoats who were blamed for the terrifying disease; rumors spread that they were deliberately poisoning wells. Hundreds of communities were destroyed, and nine hundred Jews in Strasbourg were burned alive. In the seventeenth century, the Russian Cossacks massacred tens of thousands of Jews in what is today the Ukraine. Anti-Semitism was not limited to Christians. In the nineteenth century, a Muslim traveler of the era wrote:

A political cartoon from 1898 reveals anti-Semitism, indicating that Jews have a sinister control over the world's business.

> I have seen a little fellow of six years old, with a troop of fat toddlers of only three and four, teaching [them] to throw stones at a Jew, and one little urchin would, with the greatest coolness, waddle up to the man and literally spit upon his Jewish [clothing]. To all this the Jew is obliged to

submit; it would be more than his life was worth to offer to strike a [Muslim].

In the mid-nineteenth century in Germany, Jews began to be accused of being a harmful and alien element in the nation's culture. By the first half of the twentieth century in the United States, Jews were discriminated against in employment, access to residential and resort areas, membership in clubs and organizations, and in tightened quotas on Jewish enrollment and teaching positions in colleges and universities. Anti-Semitism in America reached its peak during the years between the World Wars, when prominent Americans (including automobile-manufacturer Henry Ford, Catholic priests, politicians, and aviator Charles Lindbergh) openly spoke out against Jews, going so far as to claim that a Jewish conspiracy was controlling America's finances. These centuries of prejudice culminated with the Holocaust, when the German Nazis killed six million Jews.

Today, Jewish people consider themselves as a group to be survivors. Despite centuries of prejudice, their faith and their culture has not only survived, but thrived and continues to enrich the world. Modern Jewish organizations stress the importance of never forgetting the Holocaust. This enormous blot on the world's history stands as a terrible reminder of where prejudice can lead.

Other political cartoons reveal early twentieth-century prejudice against Jews, portraying them as a parasite preying on the world and as the "wandering Jew." Such negative portrayals fanned the flames of prejudice that eventually led to the Holocaust.

Prejudice and the Media

News reports, television, and movies play a major role in spreading and fostering prejudice. In 2005, for example, *The Sun*, a UK newspaper, ran stories that used terms like "gipsy free-for-all" and "illegal camp madness" to describe Traveler protests over land claims; *The Sun* called on readers to "stamp on the camps," saying that it spoke for millions of householders who faced having their homes "ruined" by Gypsy camps. How do the words used in these articles encourage prejudice?

Mae-Ann Smith is clearly an angry woman, but her anger makes her sad. "Does anyone remember that half a million Gypsies were killed by the Nazis during World War II? No. People remember the Jews. People feel like the world owes the Jews for looking away when that terrible thing was happening. But no one feels like the world owes the Gypsies anything. Today, Gypsies face more prejudice than any other group in Europe. It's true. Some people hate the Arabs, or others look down on people with black skin—but almost *everyone* hates Gypsies. No one wants us in their community. Everyone thinks they're *justified* for not wanting us around. They think, 'I'm not prejudiced because Gypsies really are nuisances no one would want in their community.'"

Mae-Ann waved her hand at the electric plant squatting next door to the park where she lives. "See that? The legal sites we're given are always next to things like that. Or next to railroad tracks, or in the middle of an industrial site. Places where no one else would want to live. Places that are dangerous for our children, for our health."

When asked what she would like kids in North America and around the world to learn from her experience, Mae-Ann said, "Tell them this: No matter what a person looks like on the outside, no matter where they live, or what they believe, or how they talk, or what clothes they wear, people are all the same. We're made of blood and bone. We laugh and cry. We use the toilet and sleep at night. We pray to God. We cry and laugh and love and get angry. We're all the same."

Chapter Two

OUT OF AFRICA

W ilhelmina Brown knows about racism. She's a black woman who grew up in the American South during the 1960s. She remembers what it was like to have to use a different restroom from white folks, how it felt to see a sign that said you had to use a different drinking fountain, how much she wanted to go to the "good" beach in Myrtle Beach, South Carolina, and how she didn't understand when her parents explained that she and her family could only go to a dirty beach with dangerous currents.

"When you're a little girl," she said, "living in a big family where everyone loves you, you grow up thinking you're pretty special. You know you're pretty and smart and good with words and all that. And then one day, you go out and run smack into this completely different viewpoint. You find out that there's this whole world out there that thinks you're ugly and stupid and not as good at anything, simply because your skin is black and your ancestors came from Africa. It's a big shock."

HISTORY LESSON

Africans being captured by Europeans for slavery.

Black Americans' ancestors did not come to the United States by choice. Instead, they were captured from their homes, herded at gunpoint onto ships in West Africa, and then

Slavery's History

The earliest human communities had no slaves. Hunter-gatherers and the earliest farmers collected or grew just enough food for themselves, so they had no use for slavery: one more pair of hands would have only meant one more mouth to feed. There was no advantage in "owning" another human being.

Once people gathered in towns and cities, however, a surplus of food created in the countryside (often on large farms) made possible the production of goods in towns. Having a reliable source of cheap labor that cost no more than the minimum of food and lodging was now a real benefit to the owners of large farms and workshops. These were the conditions that gave birth to slavery. Every ancient civilization used slaves.

In the ancient world, slaves came from a variety of sources. War supplied most of them; when a town fell to a hostile army, the inhabitants who would make useful workers were taken as slaves (and the rest were killed). Pirates also offered their captives for sale. A criminal might be sentenced to slavery, and an unpaid debt could lead to slavery for the debtor. Poor people sometimes sold their own children. But slavery was never associated with racial differences. That came later.

taken across the Atlantic. Conditions on the slave ships were horrific; more than one in ten Africans died on the way, over a million and a half people. Once they arrived in the Americas, they were sold at auctions and then forced to work fifteen, sixteen, or even eighteen hours a day.

Africans who arrived in the British Caribbean islands in the eighteenth century had little chance of survival; 1.6 million human beings were brought there during the 1700s, but by the end of the century, there were only 600,000 living slaves. In North America, however, the more **temperate** climate and greater quantities of fresh food gave the Africans a better chance of survival. The slave population there was 500,000 at the beginning of the eighteenth century, and by 1860, it had grown to 6 million. Still, the death toll was

temperate: moderate, without extremes in temperatures.

An Early Alternative to Slavery

At first, North American plantation owners used indentured servants instead of slaves to meet their labor needs. These individuals had signed a contract to work for three, five, or seven years for no wages in exchange for their passage across the Atlantic. In 1638, an indentured servant cost £12 while a slave cost £25.37. Since neither the servant nor the slave was likely to live more than four or five years, the servants seemed to offer the plantation owners "more bucks for their dollar" (or their pounds) than the slaves did.

This inhumanity was not based on racism. If prejudice was at play, it had more to do with the fact that merchants and those in government did not see the human value of those who were poor. At the same period of time (and for the next two centuries), "pressed" men—poor men who had been kidnapped from the streets—manned the British navy.

heavy and horrifying: 10 million Africans had crossed the Atlantic to North America, compared to only 2 million Europeans, and yet the white population was up to 12 million by the mid-1800s, twice as much the black.

Once Europeans began the large-scale production of tobacco and sugar in their North

A drawing of Africans being shipped to Key West, Florida, on board a ship in 1860.

American colonies, they needed an enormous labor force to keep their plantations thriving. White servants weren't plentiful enough to meet their needs, so plantation owners turned more and more to the African slave trade. Before long, a thriving economy had been built in North America—and slavery was the backbone that ran down its middle.

In the beginning, though, slaves and servants were treated much the same. Both could be branded with an "R" (for "runaway") if they tried to escape, and both worked alongside each other in the fields. They often lived together and spent their free time together. Sometimes they even married each other.

This drawing portrays slaves being branded by their "owner."

Skin Color and Racism

In the ancient and medieval worlds, people apparently did not regard skin color as any more significant than any other physical characteristic (such as height, hair color, or eye color). Tomb paintings from ancient Egypt show what looks like random mixtures of white-, brown-, and black-skinned figures. In early sixteenth-century Dutch paintings, people with white and black skins are portrayed side by side as equals.

What's more, the early slave traders and owners did not use racial inferiority to excuse slavery. Instead, they used ancient Greek and Roman writings that justified the enslavement of those captured during war. Eventually, however, this way of thinking would no longer work for the large-scale slave economy of the 1700s. People were well aware now that slaves were purchased from merchants who had captured innocent Africans. And more and more children were born and raised as slaves.

And once in a while, they joined together to fight back against the plantation owners.

This worried the white landowners. In self-defense, they instituted laws that would divide the Africans and the poor whites. The Virginia House of Burgesses, for instance, decreed that "negro" slaves could be lashed if they got in a fight with a white servant; "negroes and mulattos" could also be killed if they tried to escape from their "masters." And any white person who married a person of color would be banished from the colony.

banished:
forced out; sent or driven away.

On July 30, 2008, the U.S. House of Representatives passed a resolution apologizing for American slavery and subsequent discriminatory laws.

As more and more people owned slaves, and slavery became essential to an entire way of life, eighteenth-century societies needed to justify their actions. This was a time when most whites considered themselves Christians, so they turned to the Bible to find an excuse for slavery. Christian supporters of slavery began claiming that Africans were descended from Ham, the cursed son of Noah—and therefore, God didn't care if Africans were enslaved; in fact, He approved.

The economy of the Southern colonies came to depend on slave labor. This illustration shows African slaves' role in seventeenth-century tobacco production.

Enlighten-ment: *a philosophical movement in the 18th century emphasizing the importance of human reason.*

justification: *a reason or excuse that defends or explains an action or belief.*

Those white-skinned folk who had more scientific leanings (since the **Enlightenment** was also sweeping through Europe) used another (though similar) **justification**, namely that Africans were "sub-human." This meant the great thinkers of the century could proclaim that "all men are created equal," and still condone slavery, since non-whites were not men. Racism based on color was now born.

For most blacks taken to the Americas, life became a nightmare of cruelty and hard work. One slave said it seemed the fields stretched "from one end of the earth to the other." Everyone—men, women, children, old people, sick people—worked. On most plantations, a horn or bell woke workers at about four in the morning, and thirty minutes later, slaves were expected to be out of their cabins and on their way to the fields; anyone who was late was whipped. An ex-slave in Virginia recalled seeing women scurrying to the fields "with their shoes and stockings in their hands, and a petticoat wrapped over their shoulders, to dress in the fields the best way they could." Overseers armed with whips made sure that workers never slacked.

Slaves were also needed for the production of sugar.

Surviving Slavery: One Survivor's Story

"I had to pick one hundred and fifty pounds of cotton every day or get a whipping. One night I got up just before day and run away.

"I stayed in the woods. Sometimes I'd go so far off from the plantation I could not hear the cows low or the roosters crow. I slept on logs. I had moss for a pillow; and I tell you, child, I wasn't scare of nothing. I could hear bears, wild-cats, panthers, and every thing. I would come across all kinds of snakes—moccasin, blue runner, and rattlesnakes—and got used to them.

"One night a mighty storm came up; and the winds blowed, the rain poured down, the hail fell, the trees was torn up by the roots and broken limbs fell in every direction; but not a hair on my head was injured, but I got as wet as a drowned rat. Next day was a beautiful Sunday, and I dried myself like a buzzard."

When the United States was born and then expanded west, the cultivation of cotton spread as well, taking slavery with it. Historian Peter Kolchin writes, "By breaking up existing families and forcing slaves to relocate far from everyone and everything they knew," this **migration** repeated many of the horrors of the Atlantic slave trade. In 1820, every child born into slavery in the South had a one in three chance of being sold to a slave trader who would resell the child out of the area where he or she had been born.

migration: the movement by a group from one place to another.

Cotton production depended on slave labor as well.

Slave traders didn't care about purchasing or transporting entire slave families. As a result, families were separated from each other, and many would never see one another again.

Once they reached their destinations, the transplanted people faced a new life that was no better than the old one. Clearing trees and planting crops on unplowed fields was back-breaking work. Food was scarce, mosquitoes were plentiful, and people were exhausted. No wonder then that the death rate made some planters prefer to rent slaves rather than own them!

An Arkansas slaveholder wrote:

Now, I speak what I know, when I say it is like "casting pearls before swine" to try to persuade a negro to work. He must be made to work, and should always be given to understand that if he fails to perform his duty he will be punished for it.

Violence was the method used to control these human beings. According to one plantation overseer:

negroes are determined never to let a white man whip them and will resist you, when you attempt it; of course you must kill them in that case.

Under the law, these human beings were not considered to be persons—unless they committed crimes. An Alabama court made this contradictory statement, that slaves

100 DOLLARS REWARD!

Ranaway from the subscriber on the 27th of July, my Black Woman, named

EMILY,

Seventeen years of age, well grown, black color, has a whining voice. She took with her one dark calico and one blue and white dress, a red corded gingham bonnet; a white striped shawl and slippers. I will pay the above reward, if taken near the Ohio river on the Kentucky side, or **THREE HUNDRED DOLLARS,** if taken in the State of Ohio, and delivered to me near Lewisburg, Mason County, Ky.   **THO'S. H. WILLIAMS.**
August 4, 1853.

A poster for a runaway slave demonstrates that African Americans were considered "property," rather than human beings.

are rational beings, they are capable of committing crimes; and in reference to acts which are crimes, are regarded as persons. Because they are slaves, they are incapable of performing civil acts, and, in reference to all such, they are things, not persons.

The economic value of plantation slavery grew even greater in 1793 when Eli Whitney invented the cotton gin, a device designed to separate cotton fibers from the seedpods. The invention meant the amount of cotton processed in a day increased by fifty times. Factories needed more cotton—and plantation owners needed more slaves to produce it.

Black slaves lived in small houses outside the big house where the white master and his family lived. Prejudice grew out of the boundary lines that began here.

Trying to Justify Slavery

"There are few, I believe, in this enlightened age, who will not acknowledge that slavery as an institution is a moral and political evil. It is idle to expatiate on its disadvantages. I think it is a greater evil to the white than to the colored race. While my feelings are strongly enlisted in behalf of the latter, my sympathies are more deeply engaged for the former. The blacks are immeasurably better off here than in Africa, morally, physically, and socially. The painful discipline they are undergoing is necessary for their further instruction as a race, and will prepare them, I hope, for better things. How long their servitude may be necessary is known and ordered by a merciful Providence."

—Robert E. Lee, General of the Confederate Forces

Just as the demand for slaves was increasing, however, the U.S. Constitution reduced the supply by banning further **importation** of slaves. Any new slaves would have to be descendants of ones currently in the United States.

Not everyone in the United States was comfortable with the concept of slave labor. Beginning in the 1750s, more and more people began to push for the **abolition** of slavery. All the Northern states passed **emancipation** acts between 1780 and 1804, and the movement to end slavery grew stronger. In 1830, William Lloyd Garrison led a religious movement that declared slavery to be a personal sin from which slave owners should repent.

importation: the act of bringing commercial goods into one country from another.

abolition: doing away with something.

emancipation: freeing someone from the control of another.

An early photograph shows African slaves outside their dwelling.

The American Civil War, which began in 1861, eventually brought an end to slavery in the United Sates. In 1863, President Abraham Lincoln's Emancipation Proclamation promised freedom to all slaves in the Southern Confederacy. According to the Census of 1860, this policy freed nearly four million slaves (once the South was once more under the Union's control), more than 12 percent of the total population of the United States.

After the war, slavery was illegal throughout the United States—but that didn't mean that black Americans could take their place as the equals of white Americans. Black Americans had fewer educational, employment, and housing opportunities than whites. In the South especially, many whites found ways to maintain control over the black population.

Slavery tried to erase the humanity of an entire group of people. Its roots are still there, deep in America's history—and long after the ugly tree was chopped down, its fruits still poison American society. Racism and prejudice are two of these fruits.

WILHELMINA'S STORY

"My father was a share farmer. He worked the land for a white man, and he got to keep a share from the crops he grew. It wasn't like we ever had much money, but when I was a little thing, I never knew we were poor either. We had plenty to eat, my mama loved my daddy, we were always laughing. My parents were good people, churchgoers their whole life. They taught us kids right from wrong. They taught us to always do our best, to take pride in who we are, to be kind to other folk, to do what we could to help others who were less fortunate. So I had a happy childhood.

"The only really bad thing that happened was my uncle's death. I was a bitty thing, maybe five or six, when he died. The grownups wouldn't talk about it around us kids, but they were talking in whispers all the time, shutting the doors on us, looking sad and scared. I thought Uncle Daniel must have gotten sick and died. But then one of my older cousins told me what had really happened. He'd been hung on a rope from a tree in his front yard. The Klan had done it. Because Daniel had gotten mad and made

Generations of African Americans have worked the same land, first as slaves, and then as sharecroppers like Wilhelmina's family.

trouble with his boss, a white man that ran everything in town.

"Well, I didn't know who or what the Klan was, so of course, my cousin explained that to me as well. It was like the worst ghost story I'd ever heard—white-robed monsters with pointed hats sneaking around in the dark, killing good people—except my cousin

The Ku Klux Klan

Hoping to restore white supremacy, veterans of the Confederate Army founded the first Ku Klux Klan (KKK) in 1866 in the aftermath of the American Civil War. The Klan resisted Reconstruction by intimidating the newly freed black Americans and their supporters. The KKK's methods grew increasingly violent, even murderous, and eventually, federal troops moved into the South to control the Klan. The organization declined in power, and President Ulysses S. Grant destroyed it by prosecuting its members under the Civil Rights Act of 1871.

But the Klan did not remain dead. After World War I, waves of immigrants from Southern and Eastern Europe swept into America. Blacks from the South were moving to the North—and at the same time, white veterans from the war were trying to reenter the work force. Out of this tension, the second KKK rose up preaching racism, anti-Catholicism, anti-Communism, and anti-Semitism. Lynchings and other forms of violent intimidation once more became common, especially in the South. This second Klan was a formal fraternal organization, with a national and state structure. At its peak in the mid-1920s, the organization included between 4 and 5 million men.

This Klan also fell from favor during the Great Depression, and membership fell even more during World War II. But like a monster in a horror movie, the Klan refuses to remain in its grave. Independent groups opposing the Civil Rights Movement and desegregation used the Klan's name in the 1950s and 1960s. During this period, the Klan even formed alliances with Southern police departments and local governments.

Today, researchers estimate America has more than 150 Klan chapters, with 5,000 to 8,000 members. The U.S. government classifies the KKK as a hate group, a term used to describe any organization that aggressively and systematically dehumanizes members of a particular group.

was saying they were *real*, not make-believe. I had nightmares for years.

"It's hard to explain to a white person what it's like growing up black. It's not like I've ever seen the Ku Klux Klan for myself. It's not like anyone ever hit me or spit on me, and I only recall that I've been called 'nigger' once in my entire life. (But you'd better believe I've never forgotten it!) And yet, it's this thing you carry with you all the time. I think it's a little like trying to explain to a man what it's like being a woman. You may have been loved and well-treated by the men in your life, treated kind and never beat or abused—but at the same time, it's this knowledge you always carry with you, this invisible thing inside your head: you can't do all the things a man can do. There's just no point trying. And it's your job to put up with men's nonsense, to smile and work hard, and not complain. Well, being black is a little like that. It's knowing your own parents talk different when white folks are around. These people you respect more than any other in the world, these wise, wonderful parents, they don't respect themselves so much when they're around white people. So you learn that, growing up. You understand that you and all the people who look like you, all the people where you go to church, all your friends, all the grownups who love you, all of them will never have the same sort of jobs or make as much money or be as respected as the white people in the world.

"'You're as smart as a whip,' my mama always told me. 'You make up your mind right now, you're going to college.' So I did. I got a scholarship and I went to college, and I became a social worker. I grew up and I moved up North. I worked hard, and I'm good at my job. By the time I was thirty, I was the supervisor of my department, with

Three Ku Klux Klan members at a Ku Klux Klan parade in Virginia in 1922.

four white women and two white men working under me. It felt so good, let me tell you!

"What hurt was when I'd go back home to
South Carolina. 'You're an Oreo, girl,' my big
brother told me. He meant I looked black on
the outside, but I was white on the inside. He
said I talked like a white woman. That made
me mad. And then I noticed myself acting
different when I'd go to the store or when I'd
run into the people who owned my daddy's
farm. I'd lower my eyes and speak soft, I'd
hold my whole body different from what I
would have done up in Rochester, New York,
where I lived.

"Racism is an ugly, ugly thing. I've been
lucky and blessed my whole life. And I'm
grateful. But don't tell me racism isn't real.
Or that it doesn't hurt people. I work with
people every day who are angry and hope-
less, who have given up, who are buried so
deep in what racism has done to this country
that they don't even know how to begin to
get out. And all I can do is pass out Band-
Aids most days. I tell myself that you never
know what a little thing can do to bring
about change in a person's life. I convince
myself most of the time that I'm making a
difference. But some days I get discouraged.

"The world is changing. The laws are
better. People's minds are opener. But then
you run into something that takes you by
surprise. Like a white man I really respect
telling me a young boy we've been working with is 'just like the rest of them.' He

apologized, he seemed to think I'd feel better when he said, 'Wilhelmina, I never think of *you* as black.' Something like that makes you realize—racism is still there, hiding inside people. It's hiding inside me too, at the back of my head, making me believe I'm not quite as good as white folk. But I refuse to listen to that voice.

"So I guess that's what I'd tell young people. Don't be surprised if you find racism sneaking into your head, and don't think worse of yourself if it does. None of us can help absorbing the attitudes around us. But pay attention when that happens. Notice when racism is there in you. Call it by name. And then refuse to act on it. Tie it up and throw it away. Don't teach it to your children. Make the next generation free."

Chapter Three

THE FIRST PEOPLE

Gregory Long and Sheila Yazzi's ancestors lived in North America before any white people did. Many modern-day Americans call their people the Navajo, but their real name, their name for themselves, is a word that means simple "people": Diné. Greg and Sheila have both experienced prejudice since they were children.

When Greg was a little boy, he entered kindergarten knowing only ten words of English. He was immediately forced to learn a foreign language. This was just the first of many expectations that were placed on him by a culture that did not accept him the way he was; he learned to dress, speak, and act like a white man.

Meanwhile, one of Sheila's earliest memories is of white people refusing to help her family during a flood that filled the valley where they lived in Oklahoma. Her mother used a two-by-four board to lift her children to safety on the roof of their house, and then she joined them, screaming for help. Thirteen boats passed them, but not one stopped. "It grew anger in my mother," Sheila said. And when Sheila was sent to a boarding school when she was six years old, the teachers there hit her hands with rulers if she failed to speak a word correctly in English. "And this grew anger in me too," Sheila said.

When anger grows like this, what are the roots that it springs from? And what fruit does it bear?

HISTORY LESSON

If we could look down from outer space, we'd see that humanity inhabits a single enormous blue sphere—our Earth. If we divide this globe by cutting it in half from top to bottom, we can imagine hemispheres. ("Hemi" means half, and a sphere is round, so a hemisphere is half of something round, in this case, the globe.) The Eastern Hemisphere contains Africa, Australia, Europe, and Asia. People who come from this part of the world sometimes call it the "Old World." The Western Hemisphere consists of what we today call the "Americas." Once they became aware of it, people in the Eastern Hemisphere called the Western Hemisphere the "New World." Yet it was hardly new to

Despite the racism she has experienced, Sheila Yazzi is proud of her heritage.

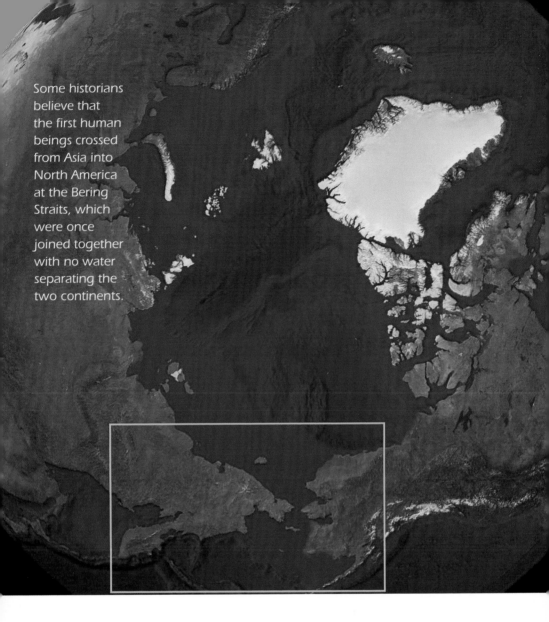

Some historians believe that the first human beings crossed from Asia into North America at the Bering Straits, which were once joined together with no water separating the two continents.

the millions of people who had lived there for thousands of years.

Who discovered this vast Western Hemisphere? Which direction did they come from? No one today knows. They came at least 15,000 years ago. Until recently, scientists felt certain people walked from Asia into North America over a land bridge that temporarily

Archeological Controversy

Not all historians and archeologists agree that the land bridge theory is correct. Some of the most ancient yet most advanced prehistoric cultures have been found in the extreme south of South America. If migration went north to south, how did people get south first? Some scientists think early people may have arrived in South America by boat thousands of years before others migrated across Beringia. Stone tools found in South America appear to be at least 20,000 years old, older than any of the commonly accepted dates of North American sites. Several groups of Native people say they originated in the Americas. Maybe different groups of people arrived different ways. We may never be able to prove how, when, or why the first people came to the Americas.

connected those continents—a narrow piece of land called Beringia between what is today Russia and Alaska. These early adventurers were hunters who dressed in warm skins and followed herds of mammoths for their food. According to this theory, they walked from north to south until they had spread out over all of North, Central, and South America.

When Europeans arrived, the Western Hemisphere was already home to hundreds of cultures, with a vast variety of languages, customs, and spiritual beliefs. Scholars estimate between 40 and 90 million people inhabited the Americas before Columbus arrived. Once Columbus stepped foot on the "New World," both worlds, old and new, would change forever.

Mistaken Identity

Columbus named the Natives of the Western Hemisphere "Indians," since he wrongly believed he was in the outer reaches of India. The word stuck. It became one of the categories in our heads, another comprehensive stereotype where we could file in a single slot what are actually many different groups of people. To this day, Native people of the Americas are called "Indians" in the English-speaking world, or "Indios" in Spanish. Today, many Native people prefer to identify themselves by the name of their individual tribes: Cherokee, Zuni, Houma, Diné, and so on.

This painting portrays the arrival of Christopher Columbus in what is now the West Indies on October 12, 1492.

The towne of Pomeiock and true forme of their howses, couered and enclosed some wth matts, and some wth barcks of trees. All compassed abowt wth smale poles stuck thick together in stedd of a wall.

After that first contact between the two hemispheres, Columbus recorded his thoughts in his private journal. The natives would "become Christians very easily," he wrote, "for it seems they have no religion." He also noted they would "make good and

European explorers to Northeastern America found the Native people living in communities like this one.

When the
Europeans
came to North
America, they
brought horses
with them.
The Native
people of the
Southwest
adapted their
culture to
include horses
as an essential
part of their
way of life.

intelligent slaves." He decided to take some of them back to Spain as captives.

From the beginning, Europeans saw Native Americans as the fulfillment for their selfish wishes. Columbus regarded them as childlike, innocent people. He assumed they would willingly serve Spanish masters.

For the natives of the Americas, this first contact with Europe was the beginning of a battle for cultural survival that continues today. Historians who study the horrific number of Native deaths that followed contact with Europe conclude that this may be history's worst case of **genocide**. No one knows for sure how many Native people died following Columbus's voyage, but an average estimate is around 40 million in the first hundred years. Although the European invaders murdered many of the Natives, many more died from diseases to which they had no **immunity**.

Caucasians had been in the Western Hemisphere before Columbus: the Vikings landed on the East Coast, and Irish monks may have visited the Americas. Yet their visits were just blips on the radar screen of history. After Columbus, for better or worse, the fates of Europe and the Americas were bound together. In the Americas, the Native people would face centuries of prejudice that continues on today. Many, many of them would not survive—but the survivors who remain continue to struggle under the weight of discrimination.

genocide: the deliberate and systematic destruction of a group of people from the same race, nationality, religion, or culture.

immunity: being exempt from or not susceptible to a legal responsibility, disease, or other liability.

Greg says, "If you add hate to hate, you just feed it. It takes one person who will not fan the fire to break the cycle."

GREG'S STORY

Growing up, Greg took for granted the discrimination he faced. It was just part of the world where he lived. He didn't think about it one way or another.

That changed when he went to Baylor Theological School in Texas. There he realized that if he wanted to be a Christian, he needed to look like an Anglo. And that made him angry. He rebelled by growing his hair long, wearing traditional jewelry, and relearning his own native language.

While he was going to school in Texas, Greg, his brother, and a friend decided to climb a nearby mountain. They parked their truck on the west side of the mountain, but as they were getting out, a group of white guys told them to leave because, "It's hunting season." So Greg and the others circled to the north side of the mountain, where they hiked to the top. When they came back down, the found their tires were flat.

"At first we thought we'd driven on mesquite thorns," Greg said. "But that wasn't it." Rocks had been put in the tires' air valves.

The same guys they'd seen before drove up beside them. "Didn't we tell you to leave?" the white men shouted.

"If you want us to leave," Greg said, "we need a pump for the tires. Can you loan us one?"

The carload of men took Greg with them to a nearby ranch, where they promised to loan him an air pump. When Greg got out of the car, though, men with rifles surrounded him.

A guy with a 45 Colt jabbed Greg in the chest with his finger. "Don't you know that in the state of Texas I can shoot you legally if you're on my property?" The man stood so close Greg could feel his breath. "This land is my land, my family's land. My father and my grandfather owned this land and they gave it to me."

Greg said, "This land knows me. Countless lives of my people were lost defending this land. Why can't I go on this mountain?"

Eventually, the men backed down. They drove Greg back to his truck, where they put air in his tires. Before Greg and his friends could drive away, though, a sheriff drove up and took them with him to the courthouse. They sat there for two hours and were finally released. "Don't mess with the law again," the sheriff told them.

"This was my wake-up call," Greg says. "I realized that the law upholds racism. The law is used as a weapon to subject Native people. The United States is a government that declares itself free, but it prohibits its First People's freedom. This prohibition is racism. How can we cope with laws and **institutions** that protect human selfishness?"

institutions: public, often charitable or educational, organizations or establishments.

But Greg does not want to let his anger rule his life. "The root of discrimination has spread throughout all humanity, across gender, class, and ethnicity. . . . Racism is driven

by hatred. If you push it, it pushes back." Greg's anger and bitterness are clear in his voice, but he acknowledges, "If you add hate to hate, you just feed it. It takes one person who will not fan the fire to break the cycle." This is easier said than done, though. Greg has learned this difficult lesson, but as he says, "Now there's the doing."

Greg's goal, he says, is to "learn from the past and build something new." He is working

Greg's artwork contains the traditional images of his people.

The Diné compass star honors all directions, all people. It symbolizes that all are needed in order for balance and harmony to be achieved.

to build a church that will weld together into one the roots of his own people's faith and that of Christianity and Judaism.

Greg also channels his anger into his creative work. He writes, and he creates

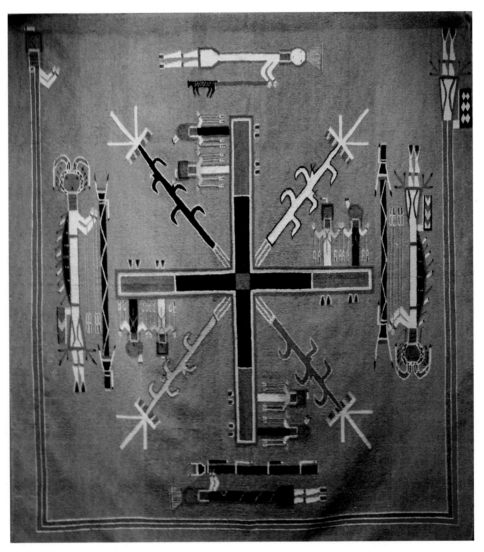

This Navajo rug contains many traditional symbols that are important to Navajo spirituality: the four directions; the colors red, yellow, blue, and black; and the corn stalks that symbolize the Earth's fertility and abundance.

paintings and feathered war caps to give to National Guardsmen, **affirming** their courage and integrity. The concept of being a warrior is important to Greg, and he weaves his

affirming: supporting; declaring to be true.

people's traditional warrior imagery into his artwork. One **motif** is particularly meaningful to him: the Diné compass star. The star contains white and yellow points—symbolizing the feminine impulse toward peace—and blue and black—symbolizing the masculine impulse toward anger and war; together these two impulses balance each other.

Greg thinks of himself as a warrior, an identity he defines as "a standpoint from which

This traditional feathered war cap, made by Greg, symbolizes his commitment to be a warrior for peace.

you do not **deviate** to gain peace." Just as his ancestors did, Greg believes he has "earned his feathers," and now, he says, "my battle-field is education. . . . In my writing and my art, I use warrior imagery to work toward peace. I am using words to create something bigger and better. One day we will all speak a common language."

What would Greg tell the young adults who read this book? "Don't believe anything and everything you see and hear. Adults aren't always right. Be open. Do not close your mind. Once you develop a closed mind, you shut yourself off from opportunities that could enrich you for your entire life.

"Don't react quick," he continues. "Seek out a person's deeper intentions. Give people the benefit of the doubt. Or you will become your own worst enemy. People are just peo-ple. We are all the same."

deviate: to turn away from.

Chapter Four

SHIFTING BORDERS

I f you were to travel down a narrow dirt road in the Carneros region of Napa Valley, you'd find yourself at Ceja Vineyards: a handful of hacienda-style houses scattered between the vineyards. Pedro Ceja's family works and lives here together.

As you arrive, a rough-coated dog with ice blue eyes runs up to greet you; he looks like a combination of husky and coyote. Get out of the car now, walk around the largest building. There you'll find a huge olive tree and a man vacuuming up olives from the ground. He's the gardener, you think, or a member of the ground's crew. But then he turns off the vacuum and introduces himself.

This is Pedro Ceja, the owner of Ceja Vineyards. He owns the place, he runs the place, he cares for and cleans the place; he and his

Pedro Cejas examines the grapes growing on his vineyard in Napa Valley, California

family do it all. They make good money and have won numerous awards for their wines, but they remain hard-working people who remember their roots. And as Mexican Americans, they know what racism feels like.

HISTORY LESSON

Things went a little differently in the Spanish colonies than they did in the English colonies to the north and east. Despite the Spaniards' reputation for cold-hearted cruelty, they did not completely wipe out entire civilizations the way the Englishmen had. Instead, the Spanish readily adopted whatever elements of Native society were com-

compatible: able to exist together; consistent.

patible with their own, leaving the basic culture in place.

What's more, few Spanish women accompanied the **conquistadors**, so many Spanish men turned to Native women as their mates. Although they certainly had their share of prejudices, the Spanish, unlike the English, were accustomed to a society where dark-skinned people (the Islamic Moors, originally from Africa) mixed freely with those with lighter skin; as a result, not as much **stigma** was attached to intermarriage.

The Spaniards in Mexico blended with the Native people to create an entirely new culture. And the land of Mexico reached far north of its modern-day borders. Eventually, by the nineteenth century, the leader of this

conquistadors: the 16th-century Spanish conquerors of Mexico, Central America, and Peru.

stigma: a mark of disgrace or shame.

This map shows how much of what is now the United States was once considered Spanish territory.

land was a young mixed-blood officer named Antonio Lopez de Santa Anna.

ONGOING CONFLICT

Santa Anna's original goal was to rid the country of all pureblood Spaniards; he felt they'd been in control way too long, and it was time for Mexico's own people to be in charge. As Santa Anna's ambition grew, he began seizing more and more power. He appointed himself president and was in and out of office eleven times between 1833 and 1855.

Meanwhile, as settlers from the United States began moving into northern Mexico, they talked of establishing their own country, independent of Mexico. By 1834, the Americans outnumbered the Mexicans in the northern part of Mexico. In 1835, these settlers declared their independence.

But Santa Anna was never one to give in without a fight. He attacked the Americans at the Alamo, defeating them soundly. At a later battle in San Jacinto, however, the Americans defeated the Mexicans and captured Santa Anna. Santa Anna was forced to sign the Velasco Agreement in 1836, giving northern Mexico its freedom.

exiled: banished or sent away from one's native country.

limbo: an intermediate or transitional place between other places.

Mexico, furious over this loss, **exiled** Santa Anna and refused to recognize the Velasco Agreement. For nine years, this area in northern Mexico was in **limbo**. It considered itself a free state, but Mexico still considered it part of their country. Finally, the United States admitted the land into the Union, and it became the state of Texas.

In response, Mexico declared war on the United States. The Mexican government **reconciled** with Santa Anna, and asked him to lead the war against the United States. The United States troops, led by General Zachary Taylor, were better prepared for battle than the Mexicans, and American forces captured Mexico City on September 14, 1847; the Mexican American war was officially over on February 2, 1848, when the Treaty of Guadalupe Hidalgo was signed. This treaty called for Mexico to turn over all land north of the Rio Grande River (Texas), as well as all the land from the Gila River to the Pacific Ocean (what is now California, Nevada, Utah, and Arizona, as well as parts of Wyoming, Colorado, and New Mexico).

reconciled: brought into agreement or harmony.

Santa Anna's military losses helped determine the fate of Mexican Americans today.

Despite Santa Anna's military failures, Mexico allowed him to name himself dictator of Mexico. In order to raise funds for the military, he sold additional land to the United States—a piece of Mexico along the Gila River (present-day Arizona and New Mexico). This deal, called the Gadsden Purchase, was the last major change of Mexican boundary lines. Mexico had lost over 50 percent of its territory to the United States in just a few short years.

Whether they now lived in the United States or south of the new boundary lines, the years that followed were hard ones for the Mexican people. North of the border, in the United States, Mexicans now faced both prejudice and poverty in the same land that had once been their own.

A HISTORY OF MIGRATION

By the twenty-first century, American jobs paid about eight times as much as those in Mexico. This served as a powerful lure to Mexico's poverty-stricken people, and many Mexicans flooded across the border (both legally and illegally) to find jobs on America's farms and in its factories. "So long as a worker in Mexico earns $5 per day and a

Coyotes

People who make their living smuggling Mexicans into the United States are called coyotes. Many of these individuals have organized systems that may include fleets of trucks or buses, secret hideouts, counterfeit documents for the workers, and guides that lead illegal Mexicans across the border through treacherous rural terrain. Some coyotes are unscrupulous, and busloads of illegal immigrants have been found dead, suffocated in crowded vehicles that lack adequate ventilation and cooling.

Undocumented Aliens

No one knows exactly how many undocumented aliens are in the United States. During the 1990s, experts guessed that there were probably somewhere between one and two million—and between 55 and 65 percent of these are Mexicans. They make up nearly 10 percent of America's population of Mexican descent.

In the 1950s up through the 1980s, most of these illegal aliens found work as farm workers, but today that situation has changed. Today, more and more skilled workers from Mexican cities are seeking industrial and urban jobs. Many undocumented Mexicans work in hotels, restaurants, car washes, and health-care centers.

worker in the United States earns $60, immigration problems will continue," Mexican President Vincente Fox said soon after he was elected in 2000.

The flow of immigrants looking for work across the border is not a new **phenomenon**. Today's numbers may be higher than ever before, but for the past century, Mexican Americans have been a major part of the American workforce.

phenomenon: an observable fact, occurrence, or circumstance.

During the World Wars, the American government's Bracero Program brought thousands of Mexicans into the United States as temporary workers to replace the American employees who had gone to war. However, these workers were not authorized to stay in the country, and many were mistreated and paid extremely low wages.

Crossing the border into the United States can be dangerous. These crosses along the border mark the deaths of those who never made it safely to the other side.

Immigration from Mexico to the United States has been a controversial issue for many years, and it has grown more heated recently. Many people believe that anti-immigration movements are motivated by racism. Others, however, disagree, insisting that a nation's responsibility is to protect its own citizens from outsiders. Here, protestors speak out for immigration rights for Mexicans.

Despite this, many of the Braceros did not return to Mexico. The U.S. and Mexican governments realized that the "temporary" admission of workers into the United States had not worked out the way it was intended. Many farmers became dependent on the inexpensive migrant workers and stopped trying to fill positions on their farms with more expensive local workers—and despite the low pay, workers and their families became dependent on the income provided by the farmers. Their wages were often so low, however, that some people compared the program to government-approved slavery. Faced with such problems, the program was ended in 1964.

But the flood of workers from Mexico did not ebb. Between 1945 and 1955, some 7.5 million acres of new farmland had gone into production in America's western states— and the landowners needed workers. Smuggling **undocumented** workers into the United States became a **lucrative** business.

Today, anti-immigration **sentiments** are strong in many areas of the United States. Most Americans forget that many Mexicans called the Southwest their homes long before the white-skinned Europeans came along. Unfortunately, prejudice is alive and well in the United States.

Despite this, young people, especially young men, continue to head north across the border from Mexico. If they are caught and sent back, they will try again. In the

Mexican Wages *Minus benefits, take-home pay in Mexico averages $5 per day. That's less than the U.S. minimum hourly wage.*

undocumented: lacking written evidence; lacking necessary documents, such as immigration papers.

lucrative: profitable; making money.

sentiments: thoughts, feelings, or attitudes, generally based more on emotions than on reason.

United States they face prejudice—but they are strong and eager to work. It doesn't look like one of the greatest global migrations of modern times will end any time soon.

For many years, Mexicans have been the ones to pick America's fruit and vegetables.

The economies of the United States and Mexico are tangled together. Unsnarling the situation has proved to be too difficult for either government. Businesses in the United

States depend on Mexican workers who are willing to take the lowest paying jobs, positions that few Anglo-Americans will accept.

Many American citizens resent these workers who come across the border. Americans fear that undocumented workers will take jobs away from Americans during a time when there are already not enough jobs to go around. Economics is a complicated subject, but experts tend to agree that Mexican workers actually have a positive effect on the American economy. Americans' resentment probably has more to do with prejudice than with actual economic hardships.

Ironically, Americans have always stereotyped Mexicans as lazy. The image of the napping Mexican in a big sombrero beneath a cactus is one that most Americans have seen. The reality is far different, for much of America's industry has been built on the energy and determination of Mexican workers. But prejudice is a hard enemy to fight.

PEDRO CEJA'S STORY

Pedro has lived in the United States for fifty-five years, but he grew up in Aguilla in the Mexican state of Michoacan. He came from a large family—six brothers and three sisters—and his father was a migrant farmer who "followed the crops" across the border in the United States, from south to north. He would work nine to eleven months, then come back to Mexico to visit his family and bring his

As this little girl grows up, she will encounter many stereotypes about what she is like, simply because she is a Mexican American.

The lure of better jobs in the United States is very strong for the people living in poverty south of the border.

earnings. Meanwhile, his family also worked; as a small child, Pedro stood by the side of a busy road, selling things to passersby.

The Ceja family moved to the United States when Pedro was young. They were one of the first Mexican families in an all-white neighborhood. Racism was an invisible wall Pedro could only look through and never seem to cross. He was an American now, but he said, "I felt foreign in my own land. I had to find roots in my own land."

When Pedro entered school, he couldn't speak English. The school decided he was mentally challenged and put him into a special education class. But, Pedro said, "All that made me work that much harder."

His mother had a vision of buying land in America and making a little village (like the Ceja Vineyards is today). So when Pedro graduated from college in 1980 with a degree in engineering, he, his brother, and his parents decided to make his mother's dream come true. Pedro sold the house he owned to make a down payment.

But some dreams do not come true easily. Both Pedro's parents lost their jobs: the steel plant where his father worked closed, and the grape nursery where his mother worked also shut down. For months after that, Pedro was the only one in the family making any money. He was twenty-five, married, with two children, supporting his entire family. In the end, he had to sell the land he and his family had bought.

The family moved to Napa, California, where Pedro, his wife Amelia, and their two children shared one room in their family house for two years. Meanwhile, Pedro's brother got a job working for Domaine Chandon, a popular and successful champagne winery. He was well liked there, and a new opportunity opened up for the family.

The Cejas spent the next seven years growing grapes from Chandon's vines; with the money they earned, they paid in installments for 113 acres. "Each piece of land," said Pedro, "is a partnership of family."

In 1987, the Cejas made their first batch of wine that was ready for sale: 450 gallons, equal to a few barrels, not enough to make any money. Their dream was closer, but it was still not so close that they could grab hold of it. "You can see the moon," Pedro said, "but how are you gonna get there?"

As the years passed, Pedro and his wife had another child. Everyone in the Ceja family was going to community college now to learn about wine. They were all in it together and they wanted to do it right. By 1998, they were finally ready. They made 700 cases. It then took two years to age the wine and get the license they needed to sell it.

Today Ceja Vineyards has an award-winning Chardonnay. The family achieved this goal despite the prejudice against Mexican Americans, despite the hardships of poverty. They worked together as a family, and

This mother and her children are begging on the bridge between the United States and Mexico. She has few options in her country for supporting herself and her family.

they never stopped believing in their own strength and abilities.

"Racism," said Pedro, "is based on economics." Mexican Americans are poor, and so they are looked down on—and because they

"We are
showing the
world," says
Pedro.

are looked down on, it is difficult for them to rise out of poverty. It's an ugly, vicious circle.

Immigration laws are headline news in the United States, but Pedro believes the controversy is based on "a lack of facts and ignorance. It's the kicking bull of every politician. The entire **infrastructure** of California would collapse without immigrants." Mexican labor is essential to the American economy. "We make the machine work," Pedro said, "and in return we are **disenfranchised** and unappreciated. We are viewed as unwanted. We are the invisibles. The people of Napa and Sonoma don't want to see the Mexicans who do their work—they just want them to do the work for them. They keep them hidden, because the shantytowns where laborers are forced to live are unacceptable to tourists. It's a nationwide problem."

Meanwhile, though, the Cejas are proud of their heritage. "We know who we are and where we come from," Pedro said. "We value our culture." The Cejas are also proud of the fame Ceja Vineyards has earned; newspapers and magazines have run numerous stories on the vineyards. "If any immigrant sees an article on Ceja," said Pedro, "they will realize that anyone can do it. We are showing the world."

The Cejas share their good fortune with others. They have "adopted" a local elementary school and fund the school's field trips and other educational services. They have

infrastructure: the basic features and framework for an organization or system.

disenfranchised: deprived of the rights of citizenship, especially the right to vote.

also donated thousands of dollars to a local high school, and they raised $300,000 for scholarships and programs.

Pedro Ceja says he chooses to "lead by example rather than through **activism**. I remember the struggle and remain optimistic. **Optimism** is the foundation; the building blocks that lead to empowerment." Pedro's advice to young people? "Educate, work, and empower yourself. No self-pity. Live under a rock and nothing good or bad will ever happen to you."

activism: the use of action, often direct or confrontational, to support or oppose a cause.

optimism: the tendency to look at the more positive side of life.

Chapter Five

FIGHTING RACISM

Klee, Jeneda, and Clayson Benally are Blackfire, a punk rock group that has toured around the world. The Benallys are much more than a talented rock band, though; they're using their music to speak out against prejudice. They're working to affirm all those whose lives have been damaged by racism—and in the process, they're building connections that can work together to protect the Earth we share.

THE BENALLYS' STORY

Jeneda, Klee, and Clayson are themselves survivors of racial prejudice. Their father is Diné, and their mother is descended from a mixture of Polish Jew and Russian Gypsy; her descendents fled to America in 1912 to escape

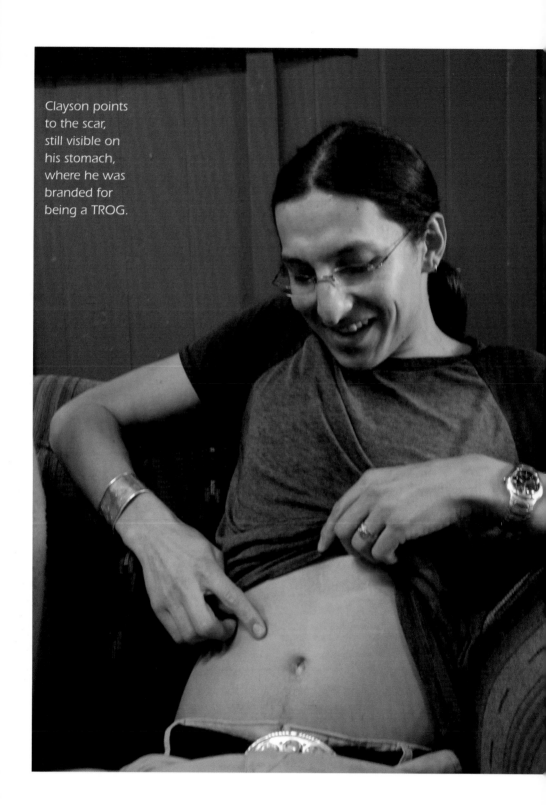

Clayson points to the scar, still visible on his stomach, where he was branded for being a TROG.

racial persecution in the "Old Country." The younger generation of Benallys has also had to come to terms with racism in their own lives.

Their first encounter with racial prejudice came when they went off the **reservation** to attend high school. "I didn't understand," Jeneda says. "I went from being a 4.0 student to getting poor grades. All the cliques were determined by race. It was heartbreaking. I wanted to drop out of school. We'd grown up in an environment where differences were celebrated rather than discriminated." Klee agrees that once he went off the reservation to high school, he was pressured to conform, to become something he wasn't in order to fit in. "'I want to cut my hair,' I told our parents. 'Why can't I?'" Clayson, the youngest Benally sibling, was also teased at school because of his long hair. He wanted to join the track team, but he was told he couldn't unless he cut his hair. Other students called him a TROG—a Total Reject of God. They even went so far as to hold him down and brand his stomach with a lighter.

"People don't want to believe it," Jeneda says, "but racism is real. There are stores where Native people don't go because they know if they do, they'll be ignored. When my father was younger, people would outright say to him, 'We don't serve your kind.' There used to be signs in stores that said, 'No dogs or Indians allowed.'"

reservation: a piece of public land set aside for a special purpose, such as for use by an Indian tribe.

pre-conditioned: prepared in advance.

dis-empowered: having been deprived of power or influence.

Racism, say the Benallys, hurts the identity of both individuals and communities. "You become **preconditioned** to accept what is told you," Jeneda says. "You see yourself as weak, as a victim. You become **disempowered**. You don't see your culture reflected in the popular media, on television, in movies, in the music, and so you question your identity."

"At first," Klee says, "you ask, 'Why is this happening to our people?' But then you move past that. You say, 'What can we do about it?'"

For the Benallys, their punk group Blackfire is a tool they use to speak out on behalf of their community. Blackfire's music brings a powerful message to people's attention.

FINDING YOUR VOICE

Klee Benally is angry. You hear his rage in his music, you see it in his face, and you understand it when you listen to his words. He has good reason to be angry—and he puts his anger to good use.

"Anger is a powerful tool," he says. "And it is part of the healing process. But anger does not equal vengeance. Anger needs to be channeled. When it becomes a negative force, something that leads to violence, it has no positive effect on anyone. When you fuel your creativity with your anger, though, you empower yourself. Positive channels for

Racism and Children's Television

Racial stereotypes abound on television, and children's programming is no exception. The turban-wearing bad guy, the brainy Asian, and the black basketball player are a few of the stereotypes reinforced in children's cartoons and TV shows. Spotting these stereotypes is often difficult for children; to them, the tomahawk-wielding Indian or the Asian karate expert is a familiar, funny character. The "bad guys" often have an accent, while the good, kind characters are usually white-skinned.

anger open eyes, minds, and heart to others' experiences. It educates people and brings awareness. Use your voice. Be creative. Find the connections between us. That's what Blackfire is doing."

As the Benallys travel around the world, performing their music in many different nations to many different groups of people, they have opportunities to share with other racial minorities, including the Roma in Europe, the Aborigines in Australia, and various tribal groups in Africa. They encourage youth around the world to empower themselves with creative self-expression. "Once you put forth your intention to address something," Klee believes, "once you **articulate** the questions, you can begin to make change."

articulate: say clearly and distinctly.

The Holy San
Francisco
Mountains.

Who Are the Aborigines?

The word *Aborigine* comes from a Latin word that means "the first" or "earliest known." Today it is often used to refer to Australia's indigenous people. Recent government statistics counted approximately 400,000 aboriginal people, or about 2 percent of Australia's total population.

Australian Aborigines migrated from somewhere in Asia at least 30,000 years ago. Though they comprise as many as 600 separate groups, Aborigines are alike in some ways: they have strong spiritual beliefs that tie them to the land, and a tribal culture of storytelling and art. Like the spirituality of North America's Native people, the Aborigines' spirituality is built on a close relationship between humans and the land. They refer to the beginning of the world as the "Dreaming" or the "Dreamtime," when the Ancestors rose from below the Earth to form various parts of nature, including animal life, plant life, water, and the sky.

CONNECTING TO THE COMMUNITY

Lack of self-respect hurts not only the individual but the community—but creativity builds communities. "Creativity is a **collaborative** act," says Klee. "It allows us to come together with others."

Klee believes that a connection to the community is vital for those who face racial

collaborative: achieved by working together as a joint effort.

prejudice. "When we are isolated," he says, "we become desperate, and desperation leads to violence, both toward others and against ourselves. Connecting our individual experiences to the community's past gives us strength. The weight of racism is too heavy. No person should have to carry this package alone." As people come together, both individuals and communities are strengthened.

"It's an easy recipe," Klee says. "Respect is the key ingredient. The first step is to articulate the justice for yourself. The second step is to communicate this to others. Don't keep it inside. Don't let it isolate you. Use your anger to build bridges, make connections, within your own community and then from your community to other communities." Communication leads to understanding, Klee explains, and understanding leads to respect. "But the circle can go the other way: isolation leads to ignorance, which creates fear, which contributes to racism."

Klee wants young people to know they can convert their anger into energy that can achieve something positive. "Confront discrimination where you see it. Look for ways to reconnect the positive circle—and break the negative one."

MAKING A DIFFERENCE

The Benallys speak out against prejudice and racism wherever they encounter it. Racism

A mural in Blackfire's office tells the story of their people. It demonstrates the power of creativity to communicate.

comes in many shapes, they know, including social racism (where individuals are treated differently because of who they are), economic racism (where certain groups do not have the same opportunities for employment and wages), and environmental racism (where a group's understanding of the land itself is not respected).

For the Benallys and other Diné, their community's rights are meshed together with environmental issues. Jeneda explains,

"**Indigenous** people's identity is linked with the natural environment. We cannot separate one from the other."

Jeneda, Clayson, and Klee don't talk about vague **generalities**—instead, they focus on particular instances of racism. They use their power to fight specific injustices. One of these has to do with the mountains near their home outside Flagstaff, Arizona.

The Holy San Francisco Mountains have a long history. For centuries, thirteen different

Indigenous: native to a certain country or region.

generalities: unspecific or indefinite statements.

Native groups have considered them to be holy land. According to Yavapai-Apache Chairman Vincent Randall, the peaks are one of the "sacred places where the Earth brushes up against the unseen world."

A group of protestors gather to pray on the Peaks. To find out more about the Holy San Francisco Peaks and what you can do to get involved, visit www.savethepeaks.org.

But Anglo-Americans have viewed the mountains differently. Since the late 1800s, the mountains have been logged and grazed, while at the same time, their dramatic scenery attracted tourists. In the 1930s, before Native

Another view
of the Peaks
that are sacred
to the Benallys
and other
Native people.

groups yet had the right to vote, the U.S. government allowed a ski lodge and an access road to be built on the mountains' northern slopes. No one asked the tribes what they thought about their holy land being used as a ski resort.

Full-scale development—with shops, restaurants, and lodges—almost happened in 1969, but several tribes and community groups prevented this initial project. In 1979, however, the Forest Service approved adding to the existing ski areas a new lodge, a paved road and expanded parking, four new lifts, and fifty acres of trails. The Native people protested that this invasion threatened their religious freedom, a basic right guaranteed by the U.S. Constitution to all Americans. The chairman of the Hopi tribe warned, "If the ski resort remains or is expanded, our people will not accept the view that this is the sacred home of the Kachinas. The basis of our existence will become a mere fairy tale." Despite Hopi and Navajo protests, however, development of the Peaks went forward.

In the 1980s, the fashion for "stone-washed" denim jeans added another layer to the Peaks' land-use claims. The White Vulcan Pumice Mine on the eastern slopes of the mountain supplied pumice, which is used to create the "stone-washed" denim effect and is also used in cement and agriculture. Pumice mining completely removes all vegetation and topsoil, destroying the mountain's natural habitats. The mining company, the

pumice:
a porous form of volcanic glass.

A piece of pumice, like that mined from the side of the Peaks.

U.S. government, and Native groups are still negotiating to protect the Peaks from any further violations like these.

And skiing continues to threaten this holy land. The present-day Arizona Snow Bowl ski area hosts 30,000 to 180,000 visitors each year. These people probably seldom consider the fact that the mountains are sacred ground; they're too busy having fun skiing. Since snowfalls are unpredictable, especially now that global climate change is impacting Arizona's weather, the resort's owners want to manufacture extra snow using treated wastewater from the city of Flagstaff.

sacrilegious: irreverent toward sacred beliefs, objects, or people.

For the Benallys and other Native people, this would be **sacrilegious**: sewage would be dumped on their holy land. Imagine how

Who Are the Kachinas?

In Hopi, the word *Kachina* means "life bringer." The Kachinas are spiritual beings, and Hopi parents rely on them to teach their children about how to live.

The Kachina dolls shown here are from the Heard Museum in Phoenix, Arizona.

Who Are the Hopi?

The Hopi live in northeastern Arizona on a reservation that is entirely surrounded by the Navajo Reservation. The word *Hopi* means "Peaceful People," and peace plays an important role in the Hopi religion. Their spirituality calls for reverence and respect for all things; their goal is to live in peace with the Earth, its Inhabitants, and its Creator. In the United States' 2000 census, the Hopi reservation was recorded as having a population of nearly 7,000.

Edward Curtis took the photograph of these Hopi children in 1905.

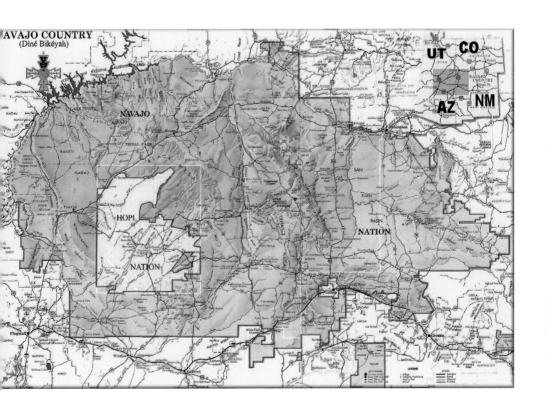

Catholics would feel if urine was sprayed on the Vatican! Or how would Jews, Christians, and Muslims feel if manure was spread across Jerusalem's holy sites?

"We shouldn't have to use metaphors like this to make people understand," Jeneda says. *"What part of sacred don't you understand? No one tells a Christian that it's silly to believe in Bethlehem—or a Jew that Jerusalem is just a myth. We are the only group who has to prove what sacred means to us."*

But historically in the United States, Native religious practices have often been considered crimes, and even today, Native people

Navajo Nation is the largest Native American reservation in the United States. It completely surrounds the smaller Hopi Nation.

seeking to pray on the holy Peaks are often treated as criminals and trespassers. "Keep your beliefs on the reservation," mainstream America says to Native groups. "The right of the public to go skiing and the right of the business community to make money," says Jeneda, "are considered to be more **legitimate** than the right of Native groups to worship and express their faith.

legitimate: legal; reasonable.

She goes on to explain, "This isn't only about our right to worship as we please, and it's even greater than our need to protect our Mother, the Earth. This is about our very survival as a people. How can we transmit our culture—what we believe and who we are—to our children if we no longer have our worship places? Our faith grows from the Earth. How will our children believe if we tell them stories about places that no longer exist? People don't realize. They don't see that this is racism."

Racism, the Benallys believe, is found in the excuses we tell ourselves, the justifications that make us feel better about the way we live our lives. In this case, what's wrong with skiing? The ski slopes don't take up all the mountains. After all, some Native groups build casinos that are just as ugly and commercial. "These are the sorts of things people say," Jeneda says. "And when you say them often enough, people believe them. The worst excuse I hear is, 'Well, it's been done before,' as though the fact that it's already

Klee, Jeneda, and Clayson incorporate the traditional chants of their father, Jones Benally, into their very modern punk music. To find out more about Blackfire or to hear samples of their music, go to www.blackfire.net.

happened makes it okay. That's like saying, 'This woman has been violated before so it's okay to rape her again.'"

TAKE A STAND

The Benallys have taken a stand for their beliefs; they're fighting hard to protect the Holy Peaks. And they're also working to educate young people to recognize the challenges in their own lives.

Racism, Klee Benally says, grows out of an attitude toward life, an attitude that says people and things are there to be used. This attitude **infiltrates** our daily lives. It tells us that the Earth and its inhabitants are there to be exploited, that it's okay to use them to make money. We're soaked in this belief to the point that we no longer recognize it.

"Look at the suffering of other people," Klee tells us. "Ask yourself, how can that be

infiltrates: passes through or into, especially secretly.

complacent: contented, unconcerned.

justified? How can we be **complacent**? How can we continue making choices that underpin the suffering of other people? We have the responsibility to take a stand when we see injustice happening."

HEALING RACISM'S WOUNDS

Before the Benallys' maternal ancestors left Russia, a man stormed into their house brandishing an ax, ready to kill them simply because they belonged to a different ethnic group. Their great-grandmother must have been terrified, but she took a stand that surprised the man. "You must be hungry," she said to him. "Won't you sit down and eat with us?"

The man's ax was bloody from the murders he'd just committed in eight other homes, but now he put it down. He shared a meal with the family, and when he left their home, he left behind the ax. "We still have that ax," Jeneda says. It's an important symbol to Klee, Jeneda, and Clayson about what is most important to their family.

"The moment we take a stand is the moment we become part of the solution," Klee says. "We become the answer, the hope. . . . Wounds do heal. We are invited to be healers—to become the tools that make a difference."

Sometimes, it just takes one person to end racism's destructive cycle.

Further Reading

Dalton, C. H. *A Practical Guide to Racism.* New York, N.Y.: Gotham, 2008.

Iverson, Peter. *Diné: A History of the Navajos.* Albuquerque, N.M.: University of New Mexico Press, 2002.

Rattansi, Alan. *Racism: A Very Short Introduction.* New York, N.Y.: Oxford University Press, 2007.

Regis, Frankye. *A Voice from the Civil Rights Era.* Westport, Conn.: Greenwood Press, 2004.

Sanna, Ellyn. *Mexican Americans' Role in the United States: A History of Pride, a Future of Hope.* Philadelphia, Penn.: Mason Crest, 2005.

Schneider, Dorothy and Carl J. Schneider. *Slavery in America: From Colonial Times to the Civil War: An Eyewitness History.* New York, N.Y.: Facts on File, 2000.

Stewart, Sheila. *We Shall Never Forget: Survivors of the Holocaust.* Philadelphia, Penn.: Mason Crest, 2009.

Yoors, Jan. *Life Among the Gypsies.* New York, N.Y.: Monacelli, 2004.

Zullo, Alan and Mara Bovsun. *Survivors: True Stories of Children in the Holocaust.* New York, N.Y.: Scholastic, 2005.

For More Information

Blackfire
www.blackfire.net

Gypsies in the United States
www.smithsonianeducation.org/migrations/
gyp/gypstart.html

History and Way of Life of Gypsies
www.umd.umich.edu/casl/hum/eng/
classes/434/charweb/HISTORYO.htm

Indigenous Action Media
www.indigenousaction.org

Save the Peaks
www.savethepeaks.org

The Snowbowl Effect: When Recreation and Culture Collide. Benally, Klee, director, Indigenous Action Media, 2006. DVD available from www.akpress.org/2006/items/
snowbowleffectdvd

The United States Holocaust Museum
www.ushmm.org

Bibliography

Constantakis, Sara. "History and Way of Life of Gypsies." www.umd.umich.edu/casl/hum/eng/classes/434/charweb/HISTORYO.htm, accessed September 19, 2008.

Farley, John E. *Majority-Minority Relations*, 5th ed. Upper Saddle River, N.J.: Prentice Hall, 2005.

Finkenbine, Roy E. *Source of the African-American Past: Primary Sources in American History.* New York, N.Y.: Longman, 1997.

Glenn, Edna, John R. Wunder, Willard Hughes Rollings, and C. L. Martin, eds. *Hopi Nation: Essays on Indigenous Art, Culture, History, and Law*. Digital Commons, digitalcommons.unl.edu/hopination, 2006.

Gomez-Peña, Guillermo. *Dangerous Border Crossers: The Artist Talks Back.* New York, N.Y.: Routledge, 2000.

Hahn, Steven. *A Nation Under Our Feet: Black Struggles in the Rural South, from Slavery to the Great Migration*. Cambridge, Mass.: Belknap Press, 2003.

Hart, John Mason. *Border Crossings: Mexican and Mexican-American Workers*. Wilmington, Del.: SR Books, 1998.

Henslin, James. *Essentials of Sociology*, 6th ed. Boston, Mass.: Allyn and Bacon, 2006.

Bibliography

Higginbotham, A. Leon. *In the Matter of Color: The Colonial Period*. New York, N.Y.: Oxford University Press, 1978.

Kolchin, Peter. *American Slavery*. New York, N.Y.: Penguin, 1995.

McNair, Adam. "Hopi." www.mnsu.edu/emuseum/cultural/northamerica/hopi.html, accessed October 10, 2008.

Meltzer, Milton. *Slavery: From the Rise of Western Civilization to Today*. New York, N.Y.: Dell, 1977.

Schneider, Dorothy and Carl J. Schneider. *Slavery in America: From Colonial Times to the Civil War: An Eyewitness History*. New York, N.Y.: Facts on File, 2000.

Tannenbaum, Frank. *Slave and Citizen: The Negro in the Americas*. New York, N.Y.: Vintage Books, 1996.

United States Holocaust Museum. "The Holocaust." www.ushmm.org, accessed October 1, 2008.

Index

Index

Picture Credits

Blackfire: p. 71, 108-109, 119

Dreamstime Images: p. 82-83, 84, 86-87, 89
  Ford, Robert: p. 20-21
  Jesse: p. 11
  Karelias, Andreas: p. 12, 25
  Neish, Nicholette: p. 17
  Nicu Mircea: p. 8

Harding House Publishing, Inc.
  Stewart, Benjamin: p. 23, 56, 59, 66, 69, 70, 72, 74, 75, 90, 93, 94-95, 98, 100, 104-105

Jupiter Images: p. 32

Library of Congress: p. 62, 77

Save the Peaks: p. 110-111
  Wagoner, Cy: p. 112

To the best knowledge of the publisher, all images not specifically credited are in the public domain. If any image has been inadvertently uncredited, please notify Harding House Publishing Service, 220 Front Street, Vestal, New York 13850, so that credit can be given in future printings.

About the Author and the Consultant

Author

Ellyn Sanna is the author of many books. She has worked as a social worker, a teacher, an editor, and a small-business owner. She lives in New York State with her family, a couple of dogs, several goats, and a cat.

Consultant

Andrew M. Kleiman, M.D. is a Clinical Instructor in Psychiatry at New York University School of Medicine. He received a BA in philosophy from the University of Michigan, and graduated from Tulane University School of Medicine. Dr. Kleiman completed his internship, residency, and fellowship in psychiatry at New York University and Bellevue Hospital. He is currently in private practice in Manhattan and teaches at New York University School of Medicine.